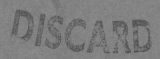

Published in Nashville, Tennessee, by Tommy Nelson™,
a division of Thomas Nelson, Inc.

Written by Earl Hamner & Don Sipes
Illustrated by Kevin Burke
Managing Editor: Laura Minchew
Project Editor: Beverly Phillips

ISBN 0-8499-1427-2

Printed in the United States of America

97 98 99 00 01 02 LBM 9 8 7 6 5 4 3 2 1

LASSIE
A Christmas Story

Earl Hamner & Don Sipes
Illustrated by **Kevin Burke**

Tommy
NELSON

Thomas Nelson, Inc.
Nashville

The day before Christmas dawned pale and cold. Snow began falling early that morning. Every red barn in Vermont was soon covered with a cold, white blanket of snow.

"Come look, Lassie," called Timmy.

Together the boy and his dog looked out the window. The only spot of color was a red cardinal which had stayed over for the winter. Lassie barked.

"Don't worry, Lassie," said Timmy. "We're going just as soon as Grandpa Martin gets here."

"Timmy, Lassie. Let's go!" called a hearty voice from the yard.

Timmy threw on his coat, hat, and scarf and rushed into the kitchen.

"Grandpa's taking us to cut down the Christmas tree, Mom," Timmy said. "Would you like to go?"

"I sure would," she said, "but Mr. Jones has a sick horse."

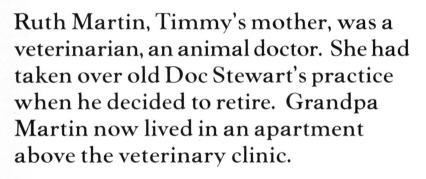

Ruth Martin, Timmy's mother, was a veterinarian, an animal doctor. She had taken over old Doc Stewart's practice when he decided to retire. Grandpa Martin now lived in an apartment above the veterinary clinic.

Lassie and Timmy rushed outside. Timmy got his sled, and off they went with Grandpa Martin.

"The day will be over by the time we find that tree," grumbled Grandpa.

Timmy knew that Grandpa Martin was only joking. Besides, Timmy and Lassie had picked out the tree they wanted last summer while they were picking blackberries.

Lassie loved the snow. She raced ahead of them and back again.

Before long, they came to an open field. Rabbit, fox, and beaver tracks told them that others had been there earlier. At one track Lassie stopped. She gave a low growl of alarm. Grandpa stopped, too, and looked about anxiously.

"What's the matter?" asked Timmy.

"Old Scratch has been here," answered Grandpa.

Old Scratch was the name of a mountain lion that was well known in that part of Vermont. He had attacked many farm animals and pets.

"Did you ever see him, Grandpa?" asked Timmy.

"Just once," replied Grandpa. "Biggest cat I ever laid eyes on. Fast, too. Out of sight before I could even raise my gun."

"You think he's still around here?" asked Timmy.

"Lassie says he is," answered Grandpa. "We'd better keep an eye open for that troublesome cat."

"How about that one?" asked Grandpa. He pointed to a five-foot-tall cedar tree which had a pretty shape.

"Lassie and I have already picked out another one," replied Timmy.

They walked deeper into the woods.

"There it is!" cried Timmy. "That's our tree!"

Lassie raced on ahead, barking. When she came close to the tree she and Timmy had selected, she stopped suddenly and growled a warning.

"What is it, girl?" asked Timmy.

Lassie moved carefully toward the tree. When she barked again, a huge mountain lion bounded out from under the tree. Timmy looked quickly to Grandpa, who nodded. "That's him! Old Scratch!"

The big cat hissed and snarled as he raised a threatening paw. Lassie stood in front of her friends to protect them. Grandpa shouted and Old Scratch bounded off into the deepest part of the forest.

"We're lucky Lassie was with us," said Grandpa. "Without her, we could have walked right up on that old cat!"

Grandpa Martin patted Lassie gratefully. "Now, let's get that Christmas tree."

It was a seven-foot-tall blue spruce with beautiful brown cones at the end of each branch. Its shape was perfect for a Christmas tree.

"It's a beauty, all right," Grandpa said. He gave the saw to Timmy.

Timmy set to work sawing the tree. Lassie and Grandpa watched. Soon sawdust sprinkled the snow, and the tree began to lean. When it fell to the ground, Lassie pulled the sled closer.

Grandpa and Timmy loaded the tree onto the sled and headed home.

When they got back,
Grandpa went to his
apartment to rest.
Timmy's mother
had just closed her
veterinary clinic
for the day.

"That's a beautiful tree," she said.

"Mom, we saw Old Scratch!" said Timmy.

"I hope you didn't get close," replied his mom. "I once
treated a calf that Old Scratch had badly clawed."

Lassie, Timmy, and his mother entered the old Vermont farmhouse where they lived. Timmy's mother helped him carry the tree inside.

While Timmy fitted the trunk of the tree into the stand, his mother lit the fire in the fireplace.

"Turn on the radio, Timmy," said his mother. "They must be singing Christmas carols by now."

A choir was singing "Silent Night." While the lovely carols were playing, Timmy and his mother decorated the tree. Many of the ornaments had been in the Martin family for generations.

"Oh, look, here's the Christmas bell
your father had when he was a boy.
It was his favorite."

Timmy gave the bell a small shake. It
made a tinkly sound. The bell reminded
Timmy of his father, who had died
several years ago.

Timmy hung the ornament with
special care. It reminded him of all
the good times he and his father
had shared together.

As Timmy and his mother decorated the tree, they joined in the singing of the carol.

"Silent Night, Holy Night."

Lassie raised her voice to join in the singing. "You've got a great bark, Lassie," Timmy said, "but you need singing lessons."

Lassie wagged her tail, and Ruth Martin patted her gently. Ruth stopped to listen when a voice on the radio said, "Heavy snow is predicted for Christmas Eve. It will build to blizzard conditions by nightfall."

"I'd better feed the deer herd before the snow gets too deep," said Timmy's mom. "You and Lassie look after the house."

Lassie looked at her questioningly. "No, girl," said Mrs. Martin, "I want you to stay here with Timmy, and Timmy, don't forget to set out the Nativity Scene."

At the door, Timmy's mom turned and said, "I won't be long."

A short time later, Ruth Martin pulled her truck up in front of Andrew Davis's store and went inside. Andrew sold everything from fishing tackle to canned goods. There was a pleasant smell of spices, coffee, evergreens, hard candy, baked goods, cider, and all sorts of odd things.

Andrew was behind the counter.

He was dressed in a red and black checkered wool shirt. He was broad shouldered and tall. He greeted Ruth with a warm smile.

"You're all sparkly today," he said. "What can I do for you?"

"I need two bales of hay," said Ruth. "That deer herd will starve if they have to go without food too long."

"I'll load the hay for you," said Andrew. "I'd come along with you, but lots of folks still have orders to pick up."

"Don't forget you're invited for Christmas dinner tomorrow," said Ruth. She and Andrew had become close friends over the last few months.

20

"I won't," he answered. "Be careful on the road. It's getting mighty slippery!"

"I've got chains on the tires to keep the truck from sliding," she answered. Ruth got back in her truck and headed out of town to where the deer herd lived during the winter.

Timmy went to his room and took out something he had hidden away. It was the present he and Lassie were going to give Timmy's mother for Christmas. It was a picture Grandpa Martin had taken of Timmy and Lassie last summer. In his woodworking class, Timmy had carved a beautiful walnut frame for it.

When it was all wrapped, Timmy called for Lassie.

"I need you, Lassie," said Timmy.

Lassie held the ribbon down with her paw while Timmy tied a beautiful bow.

Timmy went up into the attic and brought down the Nativity Scene. He began to arrange the pieces around the bottom of the Christmas tree. As he placed the figures of Joseph and Mary under the tree, he began telling Lassie the story of how Jesus was born.

"A long time ago," began Timmy, "there was a man named Joseph and his wife, Mary. The law said they had to go back to Joseph's hometown and put their names on a list to be counted.

"When Mary and Joseph got to Bethlehem, it was time for Mary to have a baby, but there were no empty rooms in the inn. So, Mary and Joseph had to sleep in a stable with the animals. That night, baby Jesus was born. A big star filled the world with glory."

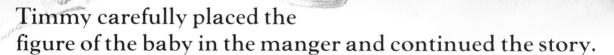

Timmy carefully placed the figure of the baby in the manger and continued the story.

"After Jesus was born, Mary wrapped him in a cloth and laid him in the manger. The manger was a box where the animals were fed," he explained.

Next, Timmy placed shepherds in the stable. "The night that Jesus was born in Bethlehem, shepherds were in a field nearby, watching their sheep. An angel of the Lord came to them and the shepherds were very afraid. The angel said to them, 'Don't be afraid. I am bringing you good news. A Savior is born. He is Christ the Lord. You will find him in Bethlehem.' Then many more angels appeared in the sky and began to sing. When the angels left them and went back to heaven, the shepherds went to see baby Jesus."

Next, Timmy found the figures of wise men on camels and continued his story. "These wise men lived far away in the East. They saw a bright star and followed it to find baby Jesus and bring Him gifts.

"Tomorrow is Jesus' birthday," Timmy said. "And we remember Him as a gift of God's love to the world."

On her way out of Hudson Falls, Ruth Martin went through the old covered bridge. It rattled under the weight of the truck and shook off clouds of new-fallen snow. The road grew steeper as she came nearer to where the deer usually gathered.

When Ruth rounded a steep curve, she could see the deer herd.

There were fifteen of them, a family which had been together for many years. While she unloaded the bales of hay, the deer came forward without any fear. They knew her because she had fed them many times before.

Before long, Ruth was back in the truck and headed toward home. She tried to be very careful. The road was more dangerous now. It was covered with a solid sheet of ice, and the day was growing dark.

Suddenly, something appeared in the headlights of Ruth's truck. It was a mountain lion darting across the icy road. She swerved hard to keep from hitting it.

At home, Timmy was waiting anxiously for his mom. A strong wind came up. The house rattled and shook. The skies had turned dark and angry. Timmy wished his mother were home.

Lassie began to bark. She went to the door and scratched to get out.

"You were just out, Lassie," said Timmy.

Lassie's ears stood up, and she whined in a way that told Timmy she was worried.

"I'm worried, too," said Timmy. "Mom's had time to get there and back by now."

The minutes ticked away. After an hour had passed, Timmy was more worried than ever.

He decided to go to Grandpa's. But, when Timmy opened the door, Lassie darted past him. She ran out of the yard and off toward the woods.

"Lassie!" called Timmy, but Lassie kept on going.

"Come back, Lassie," shouted Timmy, but if Lassie heard him, she did not obey.

Timmy told Grandpa Martin about his mom and that Lassie had run away. Grandpa grew worried, too. They decided it was time to get help from Andrew Davis.

The two of them had no way of knowing that Timmy's mom's truck had slid off the road and overturned in a steep ravine when she swerved to miss a mountain lion. Now the truck lay on its side. Quietly, the heavy snowfall began to cover the ground, leaving no sign of Ruth and her truck.

Lassie knew somehow that Ruth was in trouble. That
is why she did not go back when Timmy called her.
She did not know exactly where Ruth was.
So using her keen sense of smell, she followed
the road Ruth had taken.

Andrew was very concerned when Timmy and Grandpa Martin told him that Ruth had not yet come back home.

"I think I know where we'll find her," said Andrew. They piled into Andrew's truck and began the drive to where the deer herd lived.

The snow grew deeper and deeper. At times the road was hard to drive on because of the deep snow.

When they came to the herd, they found the deer huddled near some evergreen trees.

"Your mother has been here," said Andrew. He pointed out some hay that could still be seen.

They searched and searched, but could not find Ruth. Finally, Timmy said, "Maybe she's home by now."

"We'll go see," said Andrew.

"Good idea," said Grandpa Martin.

Back in Andrew's truck, they passed the steep ravine. They could not see Ruth's truck or the tire marks. The snow had covered them up.

Lassie was deep in the woods by now.
A sense of Ruth's danger had grown
stronger and stronger.

When Lassie came to the Green Mountain River,
she stopped for a moment. She knew there was a bridge
four miles upriver. She knew it was safer to cross on the
bridge. But Lassie also knew it would take too long to
go that way. She stepped out on the frozen surface of
the river and knew at once the ice was very thin.
Still she kept on going.

Suddenly, she heard a loud cracking sound. At the same moment she fell into the freezing water. She struggled to keep from going under. She had to get back on top of the ice. Each time the edge of the ice in front of her kept breaking. Finally, she found a log which stuck out from the bank. By crawling up on it, she was able to reach land.

As Timmy rode beside Andrew in the truck, he was very worried about his mother and Lassie. Grandpa knew his grandson was worried.

"Think good thoughts, Timmy," said Grandpa Martin, putting an arm around Timmy's shoulder.

To keep up his courage, Timmy prayed for God to help them find his mother.

Shivering and nearly frozen, Lassie kept on going. As she ran through the woods, she knew that she was in Old Scratch territory. That caused her to keep a close watch for the danger that might strike at any moment.

Even before they were in sight, Lassie could smell the deer herd. She could even tell that something had scared them.

Lassie moved toward the herd carefully. She stayed close to the ground.

Then she saw what was scaring the herd. Old Scratch himself. He was after a young fawn.

Lassie was there in a flash, barking and growling. The herd ran quickly into the woods. Lassie and Old Scratch rolled over and over in their struggle. Lassie fought courageously.

It was the mountain lion that stopped fighting first. He backed away from Lassie, hissing and spitting in anger. Lassie moved after him.

Finally, Old Scratch realized he had lost and ran deeper into the woods.

Lassie knew that Ruth was nearby, and she headed in the direction of the ravine.

When Lassie came to the edge of the ravine, she plunged down the side of it. Tumbling and sliding down the steep side, she finally stopped near a large, snow-covered mound. She began to dig as fast as she could in the snow.

Soon she came to a glass window. It was Ruth's truck. When the snow was cleared away, Lassie could see Ruth trapped inside. Lassie could not tell how badly Ruth was hurt.

She tried to get to Ruth, but there was no way. Lassie ran for help.

A search party had gathered to help find Ruth. They heard Lassie bark somewhere in the darkness.

"It's Lassie," cried Grandpa.

"Over here, Lassie," called Timmy. Lassie ran to Timmy and began barking and running back toward the ravine. She came back to Timmy and took him by his sleeve, trying to get him to follow her.

"Lassie is telling us something," said Timmy. He and the other searchers followed Lassie as she made her way back to the ravine.

Timmy shouted with joy when
Lassie led them to the truck.
But the minute he saw his
mother trapped and hurt,
he was very afraid.

The search party went to work. Lassie and Timmy
helped the others clear away the snow. Andrew was
finally able to open the door and lift Ruth out of the truck.
"She's alive," he called out.

Using a blanket as a stretcher, they carefully carried Ruth
to the top of the ravine. Soon, Ruth was on her way home,
where the country doctor would meet them.

Back at home, Grandpa patted Lassie fondly.

"We'll all have a better Christmas because of you, Lassie," Andrew said.

Timmy was very proud of his collie.

It was after midnight when the doctor came out of Ruth's room. "She's going to be just fine," he said.

Grandpa yawned and said it had been a long day. As Andrew was leaving, he said to Timmy, "I'll see you tomorrow. Tell your mom I'll bring the turkey and the fixings."

"I guess you'd like to see your mother, young man," the doctor said to Timmy.

"Yes sir, we would," Timmy answered, looking down at Lassie.

Timmy and Lassie went into his mother's bedroom. She held out her arms to Timmy.

After they hugged each other, she said, "I should give Lassie a big hug, too. She saved my life. Thank you, Lassie."

Lassie barked happily.

"Oh, we didn't finish decorating the tree," said Timmy's mom sadly.

"Lassie and I finished it," said Timmy. "Come see."

In the living room
the tree glowed with
many bright lights.
The fire crackled in the
fireplace. The room was
warm and cozy. Through
the window a beam of moonlight fell upon the
Nativity Scene. "God took care of us tonight,
Timmy," his mother said. "Yes, Mom," Timmy
agreed, "He took good care of us all."

"Merry Christmas, Timmy," she said.

"Merry Christmas, Mom. Merry Christmas, Lassie," answered Timmy.

Lassie barked twice. It was her way of wishing the two of them a Merry Christmas.

Ruth pulled aside the curtain at the window. A single star that was bigger than all the rest shone down, almost like the star that lit up the sky so long ago.

Timmy felt good. His mother was home. Lassie was home. His family was together and safe. He looked up and gave a silent thanks to God, who on that first Christmas night lit the world with glory, which continues still today.

COSITA LINDA

FONDO DE CULTURA ECONÓMICA

Primera edición en inglés: 2008
Primera edición en español: 2008

Browne, Anthony
    Cosita linda / Anthony Browne ; trad. de Teresa
Mlawer. – México : FCE, 2008
        [32] p. : ilus. ; 30 x 26 cm – (Colec. Los Especiales
de A la Orilla del Viento)
        Título original Little Beauty
        ISBN 978-968-16-8578-2

        1. Literatura Infantil I. Mlawer, Teresa, tr. II. Ser.
    III. t.

LC PZ7   Dewey 808.068 B262c

Distribución mundial

Comentarios y sugerencias:
librosparaninos@fondodeculturaeconomica.com
www.fondodeculturaeconomica.com
Tel. (55)5449-1871. Fax (55)5449-1873

[logo] Empresa certificada ISO 9001:2000

Colección dirigida por Miriam Martínez
Edición: Carlos Tejada
Diseño gráfico: Gabriela Martínez Nava
Traducción: Teresa Mlawer

Título original: *Little Beauty*
© 2008, Brun Limited
Publicado en 2008 por Walker Books Ltd,
87 Vauxhall Walk, Londres, SE11 5HJ
El derecho de Anthony Browne de ser identificado
como el autor-ilustrador de este trabajo está sustentado
en el Acta de Derechos de Autor, Patentes y Diseño de 1988.

D. R. © 2008, Fondo de Cultura Económica
Carretera Picacho Ajusco 227
Bosques del Pedregal
C. P. 14738, México, D. F.

ISBN 978-968-16-8578-2

Impreso en China • *Printed in China*

El tiraje fue de 10 000 ejemplares.

COSITA LINDA

Anthony Browne

Traducción de Teresa Mlawer

LOS ESPECIALES DE
A la orilla del viento
FONDO DE CULTURA ECONÓMICA
MÉXICO

Había una vez un gorila muy especial a quien le enseñaron el lenguaje de señas. Cuando quería algo, se lo pedía a sus cuidadores haciendo señas con las manos. Parecía tenerlo todo…

pero estaba triste.

Un día le dijo a sus cuidadores:

—Yo... quiero...

amigo...

En el zoológico no

había más gorilas

y los cuidadores

no sabían qué hacer.

Entonces uno de ellos

tuvo una idea.

Le encontraron una pequeña

amiga llamada Linda.

—No te la comas

—le dijo uno de los cuidadores.

El gorila
se encariñó
con Linda.

Le daba leche

y miel.

Eran felices.

Hacían **todo** juntos.

Fueron felices

mucho tiempo…

Hasta una noche en que estaban viendo una
película. El gorila, cada vez más enojado,
¡terminó por **enfurecerse!**

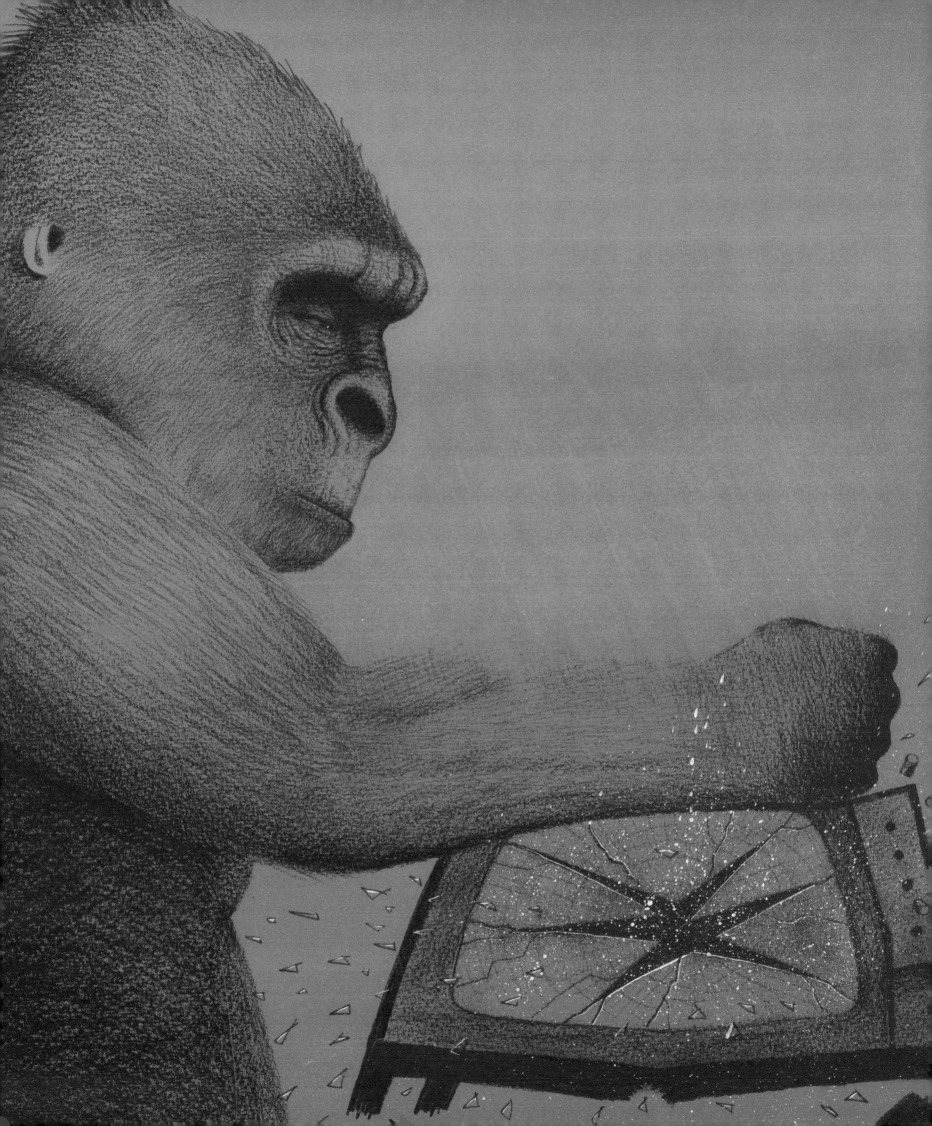

Los cuidadores entraron corriendo.

—¿Quién rompió la televisión? —preguntó uno.

—Vamos a llevarnos a Linda —dijo otro.

El gorila miró a Linda.

Linda miró al gorila.

Entonces ella comenzó

a hablar con señas…

—¡Fui YO!

¡Yo la rompí!

Todos rieron.

Y, ¿sabes qué pasó?

Linda y el gorila vivieron felices

para siempre.